マリコ　　　　　／　　　マリキータ

NATSUKI IKEZAWA

mariko / mariquita

TRANSLATED BY ALFRED BIRNBAUM

UEA PUBLISHING PROJECT
NORWICH

Mariko/Mariquita
Natsuki Ikezawa

Translated from the Japanese by
Alfred Birnbaum

First published by
Strangers Press, Norwich, 2017
part of UEA Publishing Project

Distributed by
NBN International

Printed by
Page Bros (Norwich)

Series editors
David Karashima
Elmer Luke

Editorial team
Kate Griffin
Nathan Hamilton
Philip Langeskov

Cover design and typesetting
Nigel Aono-Billson
Glen Robinson

Design Copyright © 2017 Glen Robinson

ISBN-13: 978-1911343042

Foreword
Global Spring Break

As you watch the mild-mannered, scholarly narrator of
Mariko/Mariquita shed his necktie after a three-month trip
to some mid-Pacific Islands, grow so dark he barely seems
Japanese any more, no longer use his family name – and see
his first name get shortened and then turned from "Kyojiro"
to "Koji" and even "George" – you know you're witnessing
a cultural anthropologist suffering a "sea-change into
something rich and strange" (to quote, not inappropriately,
from *The Tempest*). A "typically Japanese" man of plans is
being seduced by a shimmering, amphibious counter-world
– everything he can't understand or anticipate – and begins
to feel his identity, his sense of home, slipping away, till he no
longer knows who he is or where he's going.

Yet as Natsuki Ikezawa's hauntingly suggestive parable
unfolds, you also register that this memorable evocation of
a free-and-easy Guam is also a description of the mongrel
Japan of today. You move smoothly amidst places called
Marine Drive and Beach Park and even Micronesia Home,
unsure of where exactly you are. You nibble at chicken thighs
and corn on paper plates with a group of strangers called
Sanchez and Billy Boy and Mariko (or Mariquita). You could
be in Okinawa – or Hawaii or somewhere else in the middle of
the Pacific – but none of that really matters: you're in some
ambiguous mid-point that could be the world you know, and
could very well not be.

Ever since 1945, Japan's writers and artists have been rubbing at the same set of worry-beads: how much is Japan becoming a kind of hybrid – just another Pacific island ruled by America – and how much is it still what ancestors might have recognised as "Japan"? Junichiro Tanizaki, Yasunari Kawabata and Yukio Mishima all tried to give lasting substance to the old, in part because they saw it so threatened; Haruki Murakami places us squarely in the heart of the Japanese suburb that no longer feels Japanese at all, if only because it belongs to the Japan of right now.

Yes, Kyojiro, unsure if he'll ever catch up with the elusive fugitive who slips away from all fixities, tastes enough of the foreign not to know whether it's a lifelong partner or not. But perhaps the most alluring symbol of his arrival in a world somewhere between modern Japan and a primitive island is the sexy almost-mermaid who gives the story its name, not quite Mariko or Maria or Mariquita, not really Japanese or Spanish or Chamorra, now tender, now insouciantly in charge.

It's hard not to notice that the central two characters lose all sense of future as they drift mysteriously together. But what remains in my mind, apart from the gorgeous, lazy, tropical atmosphere – caught perfectly in Alfred Birnbaum's polished but colloquial English – is a discussion of repairing TVs. At first you think this has nothing to do with the never-never world all around it, but then you begin to wonder if it's not in fact the centre of the entire story. The only way you repair a TV, Kyojiro tells the shifting creature by his side, is by replacing the whole circuit board.

Mariko/Mariquita is a subtle and beautifully evocative fairytale that eases us into the limbo of Japan tomorrow – and, even better, tonight.

Pico Iyer
Nara/Santa Barbara

The first time I saw her, she was wearing a light blue one-piece swimsuit. There on that blazing beach, one hand on a palm tree, she looked like she was waiting for someone. Palm frond shadows playing over her slender body.

Propped up against the tree was a board painted in blue Japanese characters on a white background – Jet Ski 30 Minutes $25! Not a word in English. The board was exactly her height. She drew your attention right to it; she almost seemed part of it. A dark-skinned youth crouched by her feet, another stood down at the water's edge beside two jet skis. If her job was showing off the board, the other two didn't seem to be doing much of anything.

All this I saw from Frank's car. I was in the passenger seat and had only to crane my neck to keep them in sight. Did they really expect to get customers in a place like that? Still I couldn't help noticing, as dark as she was, she couldn't be Chamorra or Filipina – she certainly was not white. No, there was something Japanese about her face and physique. Maybe it was just the light-coloured swimsuit in the bright sun that made her face look so tan. Frank said nothing; he just kept on driving.

"Say, those people we just passed, you suppose they get any customers there?" I asked him.

"You mean for the jet skis?"

"Yeah."

"Motorised rigs aren't allowed in Tumon Bay. No motorboats, no jet skis, no engine nothing. They're all off-limits. So they do it here in Agana Bay."

"But what do they do for customers?"

9

"It's not just them hanging around, you know. One of them's in Tumon right now, drumming up customers to bring here."

"So that's how it works."

There wasn't a soul was out swimming. Everyone just drove through this stretch, car after car zooming flat out on Marine Drive past miles of wide beach and nothing inland but low bluffs and an occasional building. No one stopped. No one would think she was up to any decent work, lingering by a sign in the middle of nowhere like that. How many customers would they even see in a day?

Meanwhile I had plenty else on my mind.

The portions at the restaurant in downtown Agana where Frank took me were huge, but the taste was okay as American food went. At least that's what I told myself, considering I wouldn't be eating another meal like this for three months. I bit into the big juicy hamburger and savoured each mouthful of my jumbo salad drenched in dressing. Frank ate in silence for the most part, but then, as if he just remembered, he started in on the particulars of my project.

"Everyone's very friendly, you won't experience too many hardships. It's an okay little place, Kukuilei. You seem to have got the basics of the language down, so that shouldn't present any obstacles to your fieldwork."

"That's reassuring."

"Only, like I said before, I wouldn't be too optimistic about potential findings. When I went out there, the ceremony and all the special human relations behind it were already on their last legs. Who knows how many of the elders will still be around when you go this time? That's the real question."

"I just got to hope I'll make it in time."

"You said it."

That afternoon, at his faculty cubicle, I had Frank go over everything he knew about life on Kukuilei and the Galemumu ceremonies that were to be the focus of my survey. Granted, it was his paper written after a two-week stay over three years ago – a cursory report on the material culture of Kukuilei, with little mention of the religion – that got me interested in that island out in the middle of the Pacific in the first place.

The Galemumu was an odd mystical cult with many difficult aspects to it. He wrote me a very supportive if roundabout response to my initial letter of inquiry, along with photocopies of some simple grammar and vocabulary notes he'd prepared on the Kukuilei language. That morning, when he came to pick me up at my hotel and we met face-to-face for the first time, he limited his comments to practical details of my three months on the island.

Frank Norbert was a professor at the University of Guam, maybe five years older than myself. Remarkably reticent for an American, he'd every so often come out with some remark that had him smiling through his full face of beard. I couldn't help but like the guy.

I thought we'd be eating lunch at the university cafeteria, but he wanted to take me to this place in Agana. Probably, it occurred to me, both as a friendly gesture toward me and an expression of his own affection for Kukuilei. The island seemed to have made quite a favourable impression on him. So this invitation to a real meal was his way of sending greetings to an island he longed to visit again.

After the meal, he handed me three letters of introduction to the island headmen and offered to give me a lift to the

11

hotel, but I bowed out, saying I'd like to walk. That strip of hotels on Tumon Bay was several miles back, and the road wasn't exactly made for pedestrians, but I just felt so glad to be heading off into the field the next day. I wanted to get out and do something. I always get excited at this stage of the game. A good hike in the sun might be just the thing, I told myself. I guess it was the beer and the food talking.

I told Frank I had some things to take care of in Agana, and had him let me off at a nearby traffic rotary. We shook hands and I got out. He shouted through the window that I should call when I got back. Okay, I waved, then started walking.

The walk was more than I'd bargained for. The sun was terribly hot and I wasn't dressed for it. I'd worn a summer suit and a yellow necktie to meet this senior scholar, and by the time he showed up at the hotel lobby in aloha shirt and shorts, it was too late to change.

Now walking along the coast in my suit toward somewhere marked Beach Park, I felt ridiculously out of place. Like a salesman whose car had broken down on a country road. After ten minutes, I shed my jacket, rolled up my sleeves and loosened my tie, then mopped my face and neck with a handkerchief. Apparently I'd sweated off all the beer from lunch and now had an incredible thirst, though the chances of finding anything to drink for the next couple of miles were looking mighty slim.

Until I found myself trudging past Jet Ski 30 Minutes $25!

They were still waiting for customers. She beside the board, one of her young men crouching on the sand nearby. Though from this close up, I could see he was just a boy. There was no sign of the other one who'd been minding the jet skis. Maybe he got bored with no customers and went home.

I half-glanced at the girl in her swimsuit, but had no intention of stopping. I still had a long way to go, but then my eyes lit upon a burst of colour in the shade of the palm tree: a bright red Coca-Cola ice chest. Maybe she had drinks? I inched forward.

She could hardly avoid noticing me, strange apparition that I was, but since I was obviously no mark for jet skiing, she didn't even bother to greet me.

"*Ano*...," I called out hesitantly in Japanese. She was just as dark as she'd seemed from the car, but that face – she had to be Japanese. Or no, her head was too small for a Japanese. Maybe I ought to have addressed her in English?

"*Na-ani*?" came the Japanese response. Wha-at?

"In the ... that there ... if you've got anything to drink, could I get one?"

"Oh, that? Yeah, sure."

She ambled over to the ice chest, bent over to open the lid, and gave me a look – what'll it be, mister? I went over and grabbed a can bobbing in the ice water. Two polyethylene tanks next to the cooler smelled of petrol; probably fuel for the jet skis. The boy stared at me, sizing me up from behind his dark Chamorro or Micronesian face.

I leaned back against the palm tree to drink my root beer. A little too much to finish all at once, but not enough to take with me. Still, I had another hour's walk ahead of me, so I drank it all.

"Thanks. How much do I owe you?" I asked, empty can in hand. She was standing right in front of me. A little shorter than I'd thought. Ordinary looks, not especially attractive or unattractive – that was my impression at the time. Dark clear eyes, a determined firmness to the lips. Her hair was extremely short.

13

"That's okay. It's only one can," she blew it off.

"No really..."

"Better yet, how about jet skiing?"

"Dressed like this?"

"Can't interest you, huh?" she laughed, teeth whiter for her tanned complexion. It wasn't a come-on baiting with a free drink; it was a no-sale-but-that's-fine kind of laugh. Or maybe she was laughing at me in my yellow tie out in the blazing sun.

"So why're you walking?"

"Just a whim, I guess, thought I'd take a walk. Didn't know it'd be this far."

"Where to?"

"Tumon."

"Gimme a break. You just wait here, okay? I'll take you there."

Fair enough, I decided to sit in the shade and wait. My mouth tasted of soft drink. The boy crouching on the sand grinned and gazed back out to sea. He was very young.

Any number of cars whizzed past, but none stopped to ask about jet skiing. After a while, she came over and sat down beside me.

"So what's your name?"

"Kizaki."

"I'm Mariko."

I felt pretty stupid having given my family name, but she didn't seem to mind.

"That's Sanchez," she smiled, pointing at the boy.

The mention of his name elicited no response; he just kept looking out to sea. Northward across the bay, somewhere thousands of kilometres beyond the horizon lay Japan. Luckily for us we couldn't see that far.

"Been here long?"

"Mmm, pretty long."

I was about to ask further, when a green pickup truck came screeching up to the palm tree.

"Customers!" she announced, leaping to her feet in a spray of sand to run over to the blond American getting out of the truck with a Japanese couple. They were decked out in proper swimsuits.

For the next half hour I rested in the shade as she and the blond guy fitted the couple with life jackets, instructed them in the basics of jet skiing, then watched them take their first cautious passes; they only relaxed when they were sure their customers had the hang of it, boldly skimming this way and that across the water. If I had a pair of shorts on, I thought, I wouldn't mind getting jet ski lessons myself.

Eventually she remembered I was still hanging around, and introduced her American partner "Billy Boy." The three of us talked a while about customer turnover, better prospects up at Tumon Beach, things like that. We were speaking English, and anyway the occasion to ask how she'd come to be living on Guam had long since evaporated.

Thirty minutes later, when it came time to ferry the Japanese back to their hotel, I caught a ride with them. Bouncing on the back of Billy Boy's pickup, wind in my face as we hung a U-turn, I waved goodbye to Mariko standing beneath her palm tree.

The second time I saw her was three months later, on my return from Kukuilei. About my research findings, what can I say? The islanders were friendly, as Frank had said, all very glad to cooperate with the interviews. I was even invited to witness and record an actual ceremony. Contrary to Frank's fears, I found the elders still in good health. That much said, there were limits. In order to get a comprehensive picture of the Galemumu, a belief system with no formalised canon, I'd have to prevail upon high-ranking priests, but only common believers would meet me.

Even so, three months proved time enough to improve my fluency in the language and begin making friends – results of sorts – so I brought back a notebook of findings to Guam, along with the resolve to conduct more in-depth research in the not-too-distant future.

I didn't want to go straight back to Japan. Better to spend a week here in Guam sorting out my notes; once back in Japan I'd get sucked into everyday busywork and never find the time to organise. Nonetheless, the hotel where I found myself staying my first night back on Guam was no place for scholarly pursuits. I'd wired the airlines from Kukuilei to reserve me a cheap room somewhere, but instead they booked me at a large tourist hotel affiliated with the airline company. I was tired, so I stayed there that night, but I knew I had to move. I rang up Frank's secretary, only to learn he was in Honolulu and wouldn't be back for another two days. All I could do was wait and bear it.

The halls and elevators and dining rooms of the big hotel were filled with pale, diet-slim, big-headed Japanese couples and package tourists, every one giving off an out-of-place smell. The scent of their sunscreen, the just-purchased flowery island wear, the miniature cameras and electronic gadgets they carried around like amulets, their common little turns of phrase from Japanese TV – everything served to create a barrier to keep them from taking even one step outside the resort. They walked around as if in hermetically sealed made-in-Japan capsules, safe in the camaraderie of their own temperate kind, clasping sweaty hands in the elevator, trying to hide their uncertainty about this strange land. They failed miserably. A congress of clumsy, insecure men and travel-constipated women.

And I, on the other hand, was fed up with myself getting so irritated at them. In short, this hotel was not for me. I had to go someplace else. Three months away, it was only natural I felt this way, but whatever, I needed a change of surroundings to work on my notes. I needed to bridge myself from Kukuilei to Japan.

In the morning, I went out to the hotel's private beach. I was paying good money for the night's stay, I might as well enjoy the luxury of a lazy hour on white sand (Kukuilei had been all coral and no beach). After that, I'd go looking for cheaper digs. I hauled out a deck chair and found myself a place away from the others. Off in my corner, I probably looked the arrogant misanthrope, which I certainly was at this point. Even so, the light breeze felt delightfully cool and the tang of ocean spray in the air wasn't bad either. I began to drift off.

Thirty minutes later, someone was standing in front of me. I opened my eyes to see a young woman in a light blue swimsuit holding up a small placard.

"Wanna jet ski?" she asked in low voice, as if not to attract undue attention. The placard was in Japanese with a photo pasted on the bottom. The image wasn't her; it was some buxom blonde sluicing up a flamboyant spray.

"Well hello, uh, Mariko, wasn't it?" I said. "You probably don't remember me. Three months ago? Agana Bay? You treated me to a root beer."

"Ah, you're the strange yellow necktie."

"Yeah, I guess it was strange. I was pretty hot and miserable."

"So you're here on another trip?" she said, putting aside her placard to sit down on the sand beside me.

"Not another, I'm returning from the same trip. I was off on an island."

"An island?"

"Kukuilei. Maybe you've heard of it?"

"Just by name. Though now that you mention it, you do look a lot more tanned. Been selling stuff?"

"Hardly. I was doing research."

"Going to build a resort hotel?"

"No, not in that line of work either. That is, I'm a cultural anthropologist."

"That's a relief. That time, with your tie, I thought you were a salesman."

Believe me, rarely do I meet with favour simply because I'm an academic. We talked some. I told her a bit about my fieldwork on the island; she said her work was about the same as before. After a while, it occurred to me that she might know some cheap hotels.

"Like how cheap?"

"Well, less than half of here."

"Is in town okay? I mean not on the beach?"

"Sure."

"I'll call around," she said. And with that, she got up and walked off. I kept one eye on the jet ski placard she'd left lying on the sand, then five minutes later she was back.

"Found something. Right in middle of Agana." She quoted me a price scarcely a third of what I was paying at this hotel. And there were plenty of cheap eating places around there, so I could save on meals, too.

"I can give you a lift. I've got the car today. Just hurry up and check out."

Amazed at this sudden turn of events, I rushed in to check out as fast as I could, and exited with my bags.

Mariko drove all the way into Agana on Marine Drive in the same green pickup as before, delivering me to a small guesthouse called the Micronesia Home. Behind the front desk was a thin Chinese lady she seemed to know. And so, not forty minutes after our encounter on the beach, I was transplanted to much smaller, plainer, more peaceful lodgings. Just the place for the practical routine of sorting through notes.

"Thank you so very much. I'd like to ... that is, how can I repay you? Now that I've interrupted your day's work."

"No big deal, really. Don't get many customers this hour of the morning anyway. Mornings, everyone's busy hunting up their own kind of fun. By late afternoon, they realise they aren't really enjoying themselves, and they get the urge to do something. That's when the fishing's best."

Fishing for customers, I caught on half a second later.

"But I want to do something. Can I buy you dinner somewhere?"

Okay, I'd become more than a little inquisitive about my mysterious acquaintance. I wanted to talk, maybe find out what kept her here on Guam. Was she ever planning to go back? And to where in Japan? The women I met in Japan could all be neatly categorised; with three or four well-chosen questions, you could find out what they did, even tell what they were thinking. You could see their life plotted out ten years in advance. But with this Mariko, I didn't have a clue. So by this stage, my inviting her to a meal was eight-tenths curiosity.

"Dinner's out," she replied. "But, hmm, let me see,

tomorrow's Sunday, so we're all going on a picnic, if you'd like to come along."

Well, one day hooky from my notes wouldn't make much difference. I arranged for her to pick me up around ten o'clock.

The following morning at 10:15, it wasn't Mariko who knocked at the door to my room, but the boy Sanchez. I followed him downstairs, a pair of swim trunks and a towel in hand, and found the green pickup truck waiting out in front of the guesthouse. Mariko waved from the front seat.

"Climb on board," she said. In back was a truckload of noisy kids, boys and girls ages ten to late teens, that familiar ice chest, supermarket bags of eats, and a small motorbike. Sanchez and I squeezed in. Through the cab window I could see Billy Boy and Mariko and a woman between them.

We drove for thirty minutes along the coast and came to a section of beach maintained as a park. Someone said it was called Nimitz Beach.

Mariko called me over. "Here, let me introduce you. You know Billy Boy, right? This is his girlfriend, Joanna."

She was cute, I suppose – round face, hair curled in tight ringlets, just chubby enough to have big breasts – wearing a pink swimsuit. We exchanged hellos while the others worked on lighting the grill.

No special effort was made to introduce me to the kids from the back of the truck. Only if the need arose did we ask anyone's name. Like whenever Tom or Caroline or Sebastian or Grace came over to bring me a can of beer and a chicken thigh, an ear of corn, salad on a paper plate. Afterwards the names all ran together, faces mixing in a mosaic of laughter and salt spray and bashful sex-appeal. My name got shortened

20

from Kyojiro – forget the surname Kizaki – down to Koji, or George. I cheerfully answered to anything.

Three hours later, bellies full of barbecue, we all piled back into the pickup and drove another hour to Inarajan, where the barrier reef formed a string of deep tidal pools. Sundays brought lots of people to swim there, not just us, but happily there wasn't a tourist among them.

I took a dip in the clear water, then sunned myself on the rocks. From where I sat, I could see the kids splashing each other. I dived back in and swam a good distance out to sea while Billy Boy and Joanna sat together on one side of the lagoon.

When I got back on the rocks, Mariko came over and sat beside me. Today she was wearing a bright green bikini. She'd just come out of the water and was dripping wet. As her shoulder brushed against me, I felt a chill from her skin.

"Having fun?"

"Very much. Nice crowd. But I thought Billy Boy was your boyfriend."

"No way. He's my business partner. One of those jet skis is mine, the other's his. One ski alone's no good for business, and besides you need two people if we're going to cover Agana Bay and Tumon Bay. That's why we got together."

"So it's not just a part-time job you hired on for."

"No. My ex-boyfriend gave me the thing before he went home to Japan."

"I see."

"You're really dark. Hardly look Japanese," said Mariko, giving my arm a poke.

"I was working outside everyday on Kukuilei."

"You mean you weren't just asking lots of questions professor-like?"

"Evenings I'd talk to people. That was my work. But during the day, I'd help with fishing or planting taro, their work. Working alongside, everyone opens up and tells you things."

"Sounds nice."

"No, really, it's very interesting. Writing it all up can be a chore, though."

A boy of about ten came limping up to Mariko. "Mariquita, hurt my foot! Sea urchin sting me."

"Silly."

She had the boy sit down, then grabbed his ankle with both hands to bite on the sea urchin spine lodged in the sole of his foot and extract it with her teeth. I almost flinched, my whole body tingling just to watch, but I kept quiet. The boy was up and running in no time.

"What's this 'Mariquita'?"

"I'm Mariko, right? But Maria's much easier for folks here to pronounce. The Americans have been here for eighty years now, but before that the place was Spanish for over two hundred years. There's lots of Marias around. And the nickname for Maria is Mariquita, so ... Lately I've almost started to think it's my real name."

The perfect lead-in to ask how long she'd been here, but just as I was about to broach it, she got up, walked over to an outcropping, and dived headfirst into a deep blue tidal pool. Underwater her green bikini turned aqua-blue.

Around 4:30, Mariko found me again.

"I think I'm going to leave now. How about you?"

"Going so soon?"

"Have to make dinner for the kids."

"You have kids?"

"Not on your life. But tonight, it's my turn. I'm taking the

22

bike. If you want to swim some more, you can catch a ride back later with everyone in the pickup. If you come now, you're riding piggyback."

"I'll come now."

"Well, then, c'mon."

I got up, drawn by the mention of children and meal duty. Was she always surrounded by kids? I wanted to learn more about this Mariko.

Mariko announced to everyone that we were leaving. We both waved goobye, then as Mariko headed for the truck I called out. "Say, let me chip in for the picnic, okay? I'll pay for the drinks. After all, I I wanted to thank you, but somehow dinner became a picnic. I still haven't settled up."

"Hey, let's not make this a money thing, okay?"

"But..."

"Remember when we gave you a lift from Agana Bay to Tumon? After that, we were flooded with customers, me and Billy Boy were working our butts off for three days solid. You brought us good luck. As I see it, we're already settled up."

I could scarcely believe I had any such powers, but couldn't find the words to protest. Instead, I just helped her lift the bike down from the truck. It was light enough for the two of us to carry easily. Then Mariko retrieved a small knapsack from the front seat of the truck and pulled out a neatly folded blouse and a pair of denim shorts, which she proceeded to put on over her wet swimsuit.

"Shall I drive?"

"Why? Don't want to be seen hitching a ride behind a woman? Embarrassed?"

"It's not like that. I'd just like to have a go at driving here."

"Think you can handle this thing?"

23

"Yeah, I think I'm okay with it."

"We drive on the right here, got it? Don't mess up or we're both dead."

"I'll be careful."

I straddled the bike and gripped the handles. Mariko hoisted up her knapsack and jumped on the back. She was holding tight, but kept a space between us. We gave one last wave to the kids still splashing in the water and to Billy Boy and Joanna, then drove off.

Mariko leaned close to my ear giving me directions. We went by a different route over the hills and reached Agana in less than an hour with no mishaps. Unlike in a car, there was no way to hold a conversation over the wind. She couldn't say much of anything besides "Turn left" or "Go straight." I was aware of her warm arms around my waist, but tried to keep my mind on the road.

On the way into Agana, we stopped by a supermarket to buy groceries, then holding the shopping bag in one hand and grabbing me with the other – much closer than when she'd held on with both hands – we drove off again. Very cautiously now to avoid any spills, I followed the instructions she fed in my ear, up a narrow backstreet, turning corners this way and that, until finally by the time I was completely disoriented, we came to an alley of row houses.

"See that house where the kids are playing? You can stop right over there."

I parked the motorbike, and a cluster of kids came rushing over, throwing themselves at her amidst shouts of "Mariquita! Mariquita!"

"Hey now, dinner's coming up!" she shouted in English, as she made her way to the door, kids still clinging to her every

which way. All Chinese-looking, ages four to maybe fourteen. She told me their names, but the only one that stuck was the eldest, Chris. Wasn't he the boy who was with Sanchez on the beach when I first saw them three months earlier?

We made our way to a tiny kitchen in back and set down the bag of groceries. I took a chair by the table. There was no sign of an adult around the house.

"You'll stay for supper," said Mariko over the heads of the kids, as she tied on an apron. Very matter of fact, it wasn't even a question.

"Mmm," I nodded without hesitation, then thought to ask, "Is this your place?"

"Nope. My place is three doors down. This family, well, their mum's away just now, so another housewife and me take turns making their supper. The husband runs a laundry – but does he cook? So tonight, it's me who does the honor."

Whereupon she boiled up a big pot of water and tossed in quantities of spaghetti, then stir-fried some eggplant in garlic with celery and bacon and spices, added two big cans of puréed tomatoes and a slosh of red wine, letting it all simmer down bubbly thick. Meanwhile, she masterfully corralled the kids into cutting up vegetable sticks and hardboiled eggs, thus pulling together a simple but massive meal in only thirty minutes. She didn't even miss a beat between dishing out bowls of pasta to cue me, "There's beer in the fridge!" Obviously this was Mariquita, not Mariko, working that whirlwind of Chinese kids.

Five children and two adults around the table, it was a boisterous supper. The kids all jabbered back and forth in pidgin English and Chinese, Cantonese by the sound of it. I could barely manage to interject a phrase or two in my practically nonexistent Mandarin, but that was enough to tickle the kids. Soon they were all over me with harder and harder questions, as Mariko/Mariquita looked on bemused.

We'd almost finished, when Mariko leaned over to one boy, a fast eater now just dawdling, and handed him some coins along with whispered instructions. "We forgot to buy dessert. So he's going to go buy a pineapple," she explained.

"You're on top of everything, aren't you!" I said.

"That's right. I just love it when a whole house is jumping like this. And these kids, they're well trained. You should see them wash dishes and clean house. The only thing they don't do is the laundry, but that they can just take to their dad's shop."

"Keeps business in the family. But what does the father do for food? We just ate up everything you cooked."

"Him, he'll find someplace to eat. He's got something going at one of them. That's why the wife ran off."

"Oh, so that's the story."

"Uh-huh. These Chinese are practically all in-laws. The wife, she'll go around badmouthing him from one to the next. She won't be short of a place to stay. After maybe ten days, she'll get tired of sounding off and come home. It's not like she doesn't miss her kids. And it's not the first time either. She always comes back. Ah well ... Time for clean-up detail!"

This last phrase she said out loud in English to marshal her squad of Chinese children into clearing the table and washing the dishes. Soon the boy she'd sent to the store returned with a pineapple, so they broke rank to divvy it up. Only when everyone was good and stuffed did they wipe off the table and finish cleaning up. After that, Mariko made every child take a shower in turn, checking that each put on new underpants, then she laid down the law. "TV's off at nine o'clock, you guys.

At nine, everyone goes to bed. Is that clear?" Full stomachs and happy faces, the kids all chimed together in a great big "Ye-es!"

"Fine, let's go."

I'd have been perfectly content to walk back to the guesthouse on my own, if she'd given me directions. But no sooner had we stepped out of the house than Mariko said, "Just wait here," and disappeared into a row house a few doors down – her apartment probably – emerging five minutes later.

"Living around here's real easy going. No rich, fussy white people."

"Chinese mostly?"

"That and Chamorro and Mestizo and folks from the Philippines. There's even a few from other islands in Micronesia."

Greeting one person or another out taking the evening air, we ambled over to the motorbike parked in front of her door. This time I wore her knapsack and rode in back. Everything seemed to be proceeding right on course, but where to? I honestly didn't have a clue what she had in mind. Her driving was much more reckless than mine; we reached the guesthouse in five minutes.

"Care to come in?" I'd been vacillating between wanting to invite her in and not knowing how to say it when the simplest words just came out.

"Okay," she replied, equally off-the-cuff, parking the bike in the guesthouse carport.

I grabbed my key from behind the front desk – there was nobody there – and we went upstairs to my room.

"Mind if I take a shower?" she said casually. "There's no hot water at my place. Heater's been broken for ages, but the landlord refuses to fix it." And in she went, knapsack and all.

I switched on the TV and passively eyed a movie. Indians were chasing the cavalry.

I was trying to think what to say to Mariko when she got out of the shower. Would I have it in me to ask her to stay over? I've always been a timid soul, rarely get up the nerve to proposition a woman when I know she might actually hear me. Even if the situation scarcely seemed to require words, everything up to now had moved at her pace, and I still had no idea where she was leading. Her world was neither the standard package of Japanese society, nor was it Kukuilei society strictly bound by other mores. I just hoped I could stay in her orbit for a long, long time. In other words, I was quite taken with my Mariko/Mariquita.

She emerged from the shower, wearing a cotton floral print dress and mischievous smile. "Sure is hot," she said.

"Well, look at what you're wearing."

"You didn't really expect me to come out naked first thing, did you?"

"First thing?"

"Oh, shut up, stupid."

She sidled over to where I was sitting and sat down on the armrest, and just when I thought she was going to lean over to my face, she mussed up her wet hair with her hands, spattering me with water.

"Whoa, you're all wet," she laughed, the moment our lips met. No words necessary, I was so relieved. I tasted her lips. They were much fuller than they looked and steamy hot. I was drawn inside that moist heat.

"Hey, take yourself a shower," she said, pulling away after a long, long kiss, just as my hand crept around her back, about to touch a breast. I got up.

When I came out of the shower, she was in bed with the sheets pulled up to her neck and her floral print dress draped over the chair. I turned off the ceiling light, and with the bedside lamp still on, lay down next to her.

My impressions of the next few hours are confused. Mariko would come ramming down on me aggressively, only to curl up gently in my arms; softly stroke my skin, then suddenly dig in with her fingernails. One minute she'd be almost whimpering and the next barely containing giggles, her slender body squirming, small breasts heaving, kicking at the sheets. Then the next thing I knew, her dark eyes would be peering right into mine. We turned on the room light and compared our skin colour, judging each body part win or lose. We were both pretty tanned.

"You only slept with me because you were off on that ungodly island for three months," she said, the both of us in rivulets of sweat, staring up at the ceiling.

"I wouldn't say that."

"Come right out and deny it."

"It wasn't like that. I liked all the people out there. The adults and children and men and women – everyone."

"Well, okay, did you do it with any of the women?"

"No. If I had, I'd never get my fieldwork done."

"There, you see? So now you're doing me."

"No, no, no. I like you. I'm crazy about you."

"Why should I believe you?"

"I'll make you believe."

Round and round went the pillow talk, all through the night. I'd start to doze off and my hand would be touching something – Mariko's shoulder or breast or midriff or head. Or else I'd be awakened by a sudden shake.

"Hey, if I learned to repair TVs, do you think I'd make a lot of money?"

"What's this now?"

"Correspondence course. Saw it in the newspaper. In just six months you learn how to fix all kinds of electric gadgets just perfect. With a skill like that, I could earn my way anywhere. Open a little shop wherever. People'd pay good money."

"And it'd all go so smoothly? Do you know anything about electrical stuff?"

"Not a thing."

"Can't be that easy."

"But, just think, wouldn't it be great?"

"You've got plans to go somewhere?"

"Well, maybe I do," said Mariko to herself.

"Not for the next week, please."

"Why not?"

"Because I'm going to be here."

"Suit yourself. Still, it has been a long time."

"Since ... ?"

"Anyone Japanese."

"Really?"

"Really."

"Hmph."

I tried to picture Mariko's last couple of years, but couldn't even begin to imagine.

"Actually, it might be fairly simple at that," I spoke up after a while.

"What might?"

"Repairing TVs. These days, electronic gadgets are all unit assemblies. You don't change part by part; you replace the whole circuit board. So no real need to investigate what exactly is broken. You just keep replacing boards until the problem disappears."

"Maybe so. Maybe I'll give it a go."

"And once you've got the skill, you'll really up and leave?"

"Haven't worked it out that far."

I could feel the whole night slipping away in patches of conversation, not moving a muscle, my eyes wide open. The sun was directly below us now. Getting ready to head east toward the dawn. It wouldn't be so very long. With these thoughts, I cuddled Mariko's head in my arms and plunged into a deep sleep.

When I woke up, she'd already gone. I looked at the clock. It was after 10:00, but the thick curtain kept the room dark. There was a note on the desk:

"I thought I'd let you sleep and give you the day to do your writing. There's a fried chicken place for lunch three doors down. I'll leave my bike in case you need to use it. Drive carefully. See you around six. Bye now – Mariko"

Beside the note was the key to the bike.

Still groggy, I went downstairs to the breakfast nook by the front desk to get some coffee and a roll, which I consumed over a newspaper. On the front page was a digest of a speech by the President of the United States and coverage of a French aeroplane crash. I skipped to the last page and studied the local news and ads touting budget cars "for as low as $2999.99."

I went back up to my room, took a shower and changed clothes, opened my briefcase and spread out my notes on the desk. I needed to get some writing paper and index cards, and after asking the lady at the front desk, I went to buy them at the supermarket. After that, there was nothing else to do but buckle down and go through my field notes, copying out significant phrases and observations onto index cards. I dutifully ate lunch at the recommended fried chicken place, then returned to the room and did some more card work. Reading over each card, I tried to bring the exact circumstances to mind, adding supplementary comments where it might be helpful. Sometimes what makes perfect sense in the field becomes unclear on the page. Now was my only chance to salvage any hazy outlines from my murky memory. In another ten days, everything would fade, leaving me no recourse but to go back to the island and ask the same questions of the same people under the same conditions. Which, in reality, was quite impossible.

By late afternoon, I was starting to feel a little sleepy, so I took a walk around the guesthouse. Then I went back to my index cards. It was just starting to get dark – or rather I just began to notice – when there was a loud pounding on the door.

"Open up! Police!" shouted a woman's voice in Japanese.

I opened the door. "Okay, arrest me," I told a grinning Mariko. She pushed her way in and proceeded to detain me in a tangle of hands and legs and lips and hair, until finally we had to catch our breath. Mariko broke away and went over to the desk.

"So you really were studying."

"Of course. What did you think?"

"I don't know. Want to go get something to eat?"

"Those kids'll be all right today?"

"I popped in just now. Their mum's back. The father, too. Just like nothing ever happened."

"Glad to hear it."

"They're so stupid, those two."

Thus began another evening. We ate dinner at a nearby restaurant (better than the fried chicken place), went back to the room, and spent the better part of the night in bed. No one writes up notes at night, no one rides jet skis.

"Get a lot of customers today?"

"Sure did, a whole lot. We generally do better on days when Billy Boy rounds up customers in Tumon."

"You always take turns?"

"Yeah. But I don't got the charm. Thanks to Billy Boy's talents plus help from our lucky mascot here, we pulled in over ten people! That's money in the bank."

"Great. Money in the bank saved up for what?"

"Like I've been saying, maybe airfare somewhere. There's lots of uses for money, you know."

Why was I so gone on Mariko? I don't mean to say we weren't in the same league. It's just the problem I always have: I can never simply act on my feelings; I try to read the woman's position and suppose what she might feel, weigh the effect of one phrase versus another, build simulations on all these hypotheses. There are so many rules when it comes to the opposite sex. Like a business transaction premised on mutual assessments and counterbids. It's not just me; everybody's caught up in their own little chess game. Relationships all seem to follow this course.

But not with Mariko. She was totally unlike women in Japan. I wanted her without having to think about it, and she responded. Or maybe it was the other way around. But that was it. We both wanted to spend the night together and we did just that. There were no plans, no value judgements, no anything. Next week didn't exist for us. I was intending to return to Japan in five days. Did that make me an irresponsible opportunist, starting something so casually?

Secretly I dreaded going back to Japan. I knew from previous experience, returning to Japan from the field was a lot harder than the other way around, and I had to prepare for the worst. With me, I never get anything like culture shock on leaving. Largely due, I suppose, to the excitement of the work before me. I never have much problem with eating different foods or learning foreign languages. But going home was a something else altogether, always a trial. Thinking ahead to Japan after Guam, I felt like a child stalling in the doorway to the dentist's office.

"What're you doing tomorrow? More notecard organising like today?"

"No, tomorrow I go to the University of Guam and meet with someone. A colleague in this work."

"Hmph, so there's others in this thing?"

"Well, Frank Norbert's the one who first went to Kukuilei and learned about the island cult. I'm following up on his research. Tomorrow I go see him and report on what I found. After all, he was a big help to me going there."

"And then?"

"You mean the day after tomorrow?"

"No. Workwise."

"Well, once I get back to Japan, I do a write-up in English."

"And what good does that do?"

"What good does that do? Oh, it helps let us know there are all kinds of different people in the world. Different customs, different foods, different ways of thinking about things."

"So?"

"So if we understand that there's all kinds of people, it

might just help us all get along together a little better. If someone sticks out his tongue at you and you realise it's just a greeting, you might not end up fighting."

"Well, then, nice work."

"Yes, it is. It's very nice work."

When did we talk about what? My recollections are totally mixed up, as if it were all one big day-and-night and no dates in between. I drifted about in that great boundless twilight like a hot-air balloon while Mariko floated nearby, breezes blowing us together every so often, two inflated objects breathing low, exchanging intermittent words, whiffs of sweat and pleasure, odd wisps of conversation in the dark.

Her conversation was an indiscriminate grab bag of experiences. Which evening was it she told me about when she had to run around with a TV commercial crew from Japan? The model lording over one and all. The director growling at his assistant for not scouting more picturesque locations, the tacky cameraman who said he'd find her a good job if she came back to Japan with him. If the weather turned bad, the whole crew would get edgy, or they'd do nothing but party at night. She had to haggle to get an advance on her already meagre take-home. A disagreeable job all the way around.

"There are professionals on Guam who deal especially with these TV types, so the fact they were using me must've meant they were second-stringers. I mean, really."

But no matter how sour these stories, she always seemed to salvage some interesting boon from the experience. She'd be saying, "That's why I walked," but her expression told me it wasn't so bad for a one-time thing. She quit being a tour guide for the same reason. Tough as it was for Mariquita to find suitable work here, as Mariko she could really only do jobs for the Japanese, the best so far being her present jet ski operation. The good thing about it was she didn't have to talk to the customers all that much. Not that she made big money, seeing as they just got spillover from the big ocean-sport setup at Cocos Island, but for the time being it was all right.

"In ten years' time, I'll be somebody's wife on a small island somewhere out there in the Pacific, huffing and puffing trying to raise five kids."

"Well, you're sure good enough at cooking."

"I'm good at all that housekeeping stuff. And I'll be running the island grocery store. And you'll just happen along doing one of your surveys. We'll run into each other and have a good old laugh."

"And I'll ask you to help with the fieldwork."

"And while teaming up on fieldwork we'll fall into the sack together like now, and my jealous Filipino husband pulls a pistol and shoots us both dead. The end."

"No, while doing the fieldwork, you'd awaken to your true life's goal of doing cultural anthropology studies and leave me for a university in Tokyo. Where you make quick headway and gradually become a world authority. Meanwhile, I'm stuck back on the island raising your kids."

"Doubt they'd turn out so great, those kids."

"No, I suppose not."

I can still see Mariko's animated expression, still hear her tomboyish patter, her slightly un-Japanese intonation. One of our favourite routines was to imagine all sorts of different futures for ourselves, but she never did say why she left Japan. That week wasn't for talking about the past. I don't even know where in Japan she came from.

And yet for all our conjectures about the future, it seems to me we never talked about when we might be seeing each other again, or if we even intended to. I couldn't prolong my stay on Guam any further; one week was my limit. I'd pressed my luck with my none-too-friendly university colleagues and scraped together what I could as an adjunct just to buy that much time. No matter how enjoyable these days with Mariko were, I simply couldn't neglect my duties any longer. All I knew was this misty sense of wanting to see her again hovering in the corners of my mind. Should I have tried to pin it down?

Late in the afternoon of my last day, I decided to set aside my note-sorting and rode by bike out to Agana Bay wearing a T-shirt and swim trunks. I thought I might have one last go at jet skiing. It was Billy Boy's day to cover Tumon, so that meant Mariko would be there at the beach.

Mariko was glad to see me.

"You've got a customer," I said. "Here's your money."

"You can go for free. Let's use the money for dinner."

Chris and Sanchez, who'd been waiting around under the palm tree the same as ever, carried the jet ski out to the water. Mariko waded in up to her knees and showed me how to run the contraption. Which was simple enough, considering there was only a throttle; all you had to was let it out to slow to a stop.

I soon got the hang of it, and went racing off boldly across the bay. The faster the speed, the more stable it was. Banking into a turn, leaning hard with your whole body, you could churn up a sassy head of spray. Though if you fell off, the jet ski would automatically slow to an idle and putt around in circles like a faithful dog waiting for its clumsy master.

There were hardly any waves, but even slightest fanning wakes would be a shock to your feet and your hands on the wheel. Only once did I capsize.

Mariko took out the other ski to come after me, and we chased each other around a while. Once she came straight at my flank, barely avoiding collision at the last second. The spray doused me head to toe. Yes, as you'd expect, she was good at it.

After about thirty minutes, we headed back to shore. It'd been great, but being so machine-dependent, you tired of it quickly, too. As I neared the beach and started to feel the rasp of bottom sand, I let up on the throttle. Sanchez came running out to cut off the engine and help drag it on shore. Mariko came along soon after.

"Had enough?"

"Mmm, yes."

"You can keep riding, if you want. Until the next customer comes."

"No, I've had my fun."

I sat myself down beneath the palm tree and fished a root beer out of the cooler. As I drank it, my body still reeled with engine momentum and waves.

"So you took a spin after all," Mariko said.

"Well, that time it was just that I had on a necktie and all."

It seemed like ages ago. When I still knew nothing about Mariko – though even now what did I really know about her?

No other customers showed up the rest of that day. Eventually Billy Boy gave up and drove back from Tumon. He and the two boys loaded the jet skis onto the back of the pickup. I offered to help, but Billy Boy smiled me down.

That evening we all went out to eat together at a much

talked-about new place behind the airport. And for just
that once, the usually quiet Chris and Sanchez bubbled with
chitchat. We had dinner-size jumbo hamburgers and six-dollar
T-bone steaks with mountains of salad. We drank ginger
ale and beer. The conversation dwelled on the elusive art of
pulling in customers and the numbers that came their way
since I began frequenting Agana Bay. To listen to them, I was
some kind of lucky *maneki neko*, a beckoning-cat charm that
waved in the money.

"Say, remember those guys who ran off with the jet skis."

"Yeah, a team of two. That was an adventure."

"Ran off where?"

"Way over there, Agana way. Japanese, the both of them,
booked for half an hour."

"Paid in advance for only 30 minutes."

"For a while there they were just racing around like
regular, but soon they'd taken both skis outside the reef."

"I mean, we were pretty dumb. Stood around watching
them. Like, man, they're awful far out. But they just kept
going, and before we knew what was coming off, they slipped
through a gap in the reef and out of sight."

"That's when we got to thinking, hey, what gives? And we
went after them."

"Me and Billy Boy chased them in a motor boat," Chris
said proudly.

"RIght. Biked over to the marina and borrowed a friend's
rig. Mariquita and Sanchez went around by car."

"And?"

"And after maybe two hours we finally found the jet skis
bobbing around near the Hilton beach. The creeps were long
gone, of course."

"Stupid prank. In actual damages, we only lost $200 in rental fees – two skis for two hours – but when I think of all the worry and hassle, it still pisses me off."

"But we caught 'em, y'know, the both of 'em," Sanchez chimed in, eyes gleaming.

"Yeah, we caught 'em all right."

"Where?"

"We watched the airport. We figured the creeps had to be going back to Japan soon, so we camped out at the airport that night, and sure enough, they were trying to catch the first flight out the next day. Sanchez spotted them."

"I remembered their faces. Knew it had to be them."

"Then all of us surrounded them."

"Billy Boy laid down the law in English, and I translated into Japanese. Told them this American here was going to call the police and have them arrested. I knew that'd work better than me trying to negotiate in Japanese."

"Yeah. More intimidating."

"If the cops came, they'd forfeit their flight. Not only that, they came with a tour, so if the cops held up the plane, it'd be a big deal. So the two of them coughed up the $200."

"We just about danced all the way home," said Chris.

I really enjoyed being with them hearing these stories. I probably would have enjoyed hanging around with them to help catch the creeps, if i didn't have to creep away on an early flight back to Japan the next morning myself.

The very same thoughts seemed to occur to Mariko at the same time. She gave me a sad little look and said, "Hey, let's go," then stood up to leave.

"I'll be back. Guam's just a short hop. If I have a mind to, I can come once a month. We could see each other often that way."

"I know."

"You'll never go back to Japan, not even for a short while?"

"Japan? No way."

"Okay then, I'll write. I'm sure I'll be doing follow-up fieldwork on Kukuilei within a year. And next time it'd be a longer stay. Or why don't you come with me?"

"I'd get in the way."

"Don't be ridiculous. You'd get along better with everyone than me. Especially the children. Anyway, I'll write from Japan to let you know what's happening."

"I won't write. I don't do letters," said Mariko with a hard look, then burrowed under the sheets.

"Fine. I understand. So I'll write that much more. I'll come to Guam whenever I can."

A muffled reply came from under the covers.

The following morning, while it was still dark, Mariko drove me to the airport in the pickup. I checked in my trunk. All that remained was go to the departure lounge. My precious notes in hand, boarding pass in my pocket, I stood there in front of Mariko.

"Thanks for everything. Really, I don't know what to say."

"You take care," she said with a much brighter face than the night before.

"You too."

"Hey, y'know, I did tell you one little lie. My shower, it wasn't really broken. Well, bye now."

And with that, she raised her hand just slightly, turned about face, and shuffled straight out of the lobby. No kiss, no hug, no handshake, no tears. Mariko didn't even look back. I watched as her slim body and short hair passed through the big automatic door, crossed the street, and disappeared into the parking lot. I began to walk slowly toward the departure lounge. Next stop Japan, looming larger than life.

And that pretty much was it.

I alone knew how much I'd lost, so all the excuses I kept making after that were directed solely at myself. When we parted at the airport, I still didn't really know what I was giving up. It began from that moment, and it went on and on, slowly swelling up inside me. And there was nothing I could do about it.

I never thought I'd never see her again. After returning to Japan, I squared away the requisite university busywork, laboured to pull together my article, wrote a proposal for my next research project, applied to several foundations for grants, took on part-time teaching gigs to save up for the maximum stay on Guam, and meanwhile managed to write a good many letters to Mariko. True to her word, no responses came.

All the same, I couldn't even begin to realise my promise to visit Guam once a month. Blame it on my economic straits or the intensity of Japanese work habits, the buzzing pace of social activity – it just wasn't possible. Naturally I tried to explain these things in my letters, but my explanations always seemed more like excuses. I wrote about wanting to come over soon, wrote please wait just a little longer, wrote running commentaries on the review process for my grants. Whether Mariko would understand or not wasn't the issue. It was all I could do to write, and yet I was exasperated at my own indecisiveness. Why couldn't I just pick up and go, no matter how foolish or unreasonable? To be honest, there was no reason, either in terms of money or time. Why couldn't I have made the trip once? But somehow I figured the money I saved by not splurging would be better spent next time when I went for real. I'm a saver. I save up achievements, save up personal connections, save up future plans. In that sense, I'm typically Japanese, and therefore completely different from Mariko.

Mariko would change. I imagined her changing over those three months, the next half year, year – and it frightened me. Mariko saved nothing. She lived by changing herself to accommodate her surroundings. Effortlessly, it seemed. Which is why she could adapt to any locale, any circumstances, finding adequate new jobs and friends and lovers each time, pushing toward the future on their strengths. The result being – or rather the interim report – there had been the Mariko/Mariquita I met when I went to Guam. But she goes on changing. Unless you stayed right there with her, she'd break away. And once she did that, there was no catching up. When I saw her again – if I ever saw her again – she'd probably have jettisoned most everything Mariko and become that much more Mariquita. Which would put her out of my reach.

The next time I went to Guam was exactly a year later. The grant came through and of course I hurried to send Mariko the news. This time for sure, I'm definitely coming, I wrote, including my arrival details. I posted a letter to the Micronesia Home to book a room so I'd have one free week before shipping off to Kukuilei. If she felt like coming along for the fieldwork, I had money (out of my own pocket) for that, too.

The four-hour flight Agana got in on time, but there was no sign of her at the airport. I half-expected her not to come, or rather I suppressed my expectations as I got off the plane. At Immigration, then again at Customs, I had to fight to keep

43

my hopes from welling up. Once outside, I scanned the arrival lobby crowded with tour reps and hotel valets, but no Mariko.

I just sat in the lobby astride my trunk. Maybe something came up and she couldn't make it. Maybe she sent Sanchez or Chris in her place. Or some other new kid might call my name out of nowhere. But wait as I did, no one came.

Twenty minutes later, I cranked myself to my feet and walked over to the rent-a-car counter. Once I had wheels, I took Marine Drive along the coast. The afternoon sun was fierce, glinting off the sea with a dizzying glare. Yet nowhere on those miles of beach was there Jet Ski 30 Minutes $25! And no Mariko/Mariquita standing beside it.

I drove to Agana and checked in at the guesthouse, then slowly walked toward Mariko's house. I was amazed I still remembered the way. Not a thing had changed in Agana. The scent in the air, that twilight tinge in the sky, the sounds of life in the backstreets, everything was exactly the same.

As soon as I turned the corner into her street I saw kids shouting and playing. Again, exactly like a year before. I stopped in my tracks and for a while just watched them tossing rocks at a chalk figure on the ground.

After five minutes, an apartment door opened and out stepped a young man. It was Chris. He came walking in my direction and was about to lope right past me when I spoke up. "Hey, Chris."

"Wha...? Er, Koji?" I was happy he remembered my name.

"Yeah, it's me. Koji." I paused a silent moment and took a deep breath. "Seen Mariquita?"

"She's gone. She left."

It wasn't unexpected, but still it sapped the strength out of me.

"Where'd she go?"

44

"Vanuatu. Maybe two months ago, I guess."

I nodded slowly. Vanuatu. The New Hebrides, an archipelago dead centre in the Pacific. I'd never been there, but the name was familiar of course. It always comes up in studies on cargo cults. Why there? How'd she go about getting there? Go to Manila, then fly to Port Moresby, then hop over to Port Vila. Or else maybe via Honolulu?

I could see Mariko getting off the plane in Port Vila, briskly descending the stairs to the tarmac and looking up at the bright sky. Yeah, I can make a go of it here. Whatever awaited her, Mariko/Mariquita would never sink or capsize; she'd cut the waves full speed ahead. Not a doubt in her mind, she'd pick up the language and bearings and customs, ally herself with an entourage of local kids, everything would go fine.

And then, for some reason, I pictured myself deplaning at that same Port Vila airport. This scene was hazier, tentative. A shaky image I had to pull into focus somehow. If I left right now, I could still catch up with Mariquita. Now, while there was still time. Two months' head start wasn't that much.

Desperately, I kept turning over these thoughts. There on that backstreet in Agana, in front of those row houses, with Chris looking at me completely puzzled. I kept thinking, if I hurried I might just catch up with her, but my feet wouldn't budge.

About the Project

Keshiki is a series of chapbooks showcasing the work of some of the most exciting writers working in Japan today, published by Strangers Press, part of the UEA Publishing Project.

Each story is beautifully translated and presented as an individual chapbook, with a design inspired by the text.

Keshiki is a unique collaboration between University of East Anglia, Norwich University of the Arts, and Writers' Centre Norwich, funded by the Nippon Foundation.

Supported by

THE NIPPON FOUNDATION

WRITERS'
CENTRE
NORWICH

University of East Anglia

NORWICH UNIVERSITY OF THE ARTS

1 —
Time Differences
Yoko Tawada
Translated by Jeffrey Angles

2 —
Friendship for Grown-Ups
Nao-Cola Yamazaki
Translated by Polly Barton

3 —
Spring Sleepers
Kyoko Yoshida

4 —
Mariko/Mariquita
Natsuki Ikezawa
Translated by Alfred Birnbaum

5 —
The Girl Who Is Getting Married
Aoko Matsuda
Translated by Angus Turvill

6 —
At the Edge of the Wood
Masatsugu Ono
Translated by Juliet Winters Carpenter

7 —
Mikumari
Misumi Kubo
Translated by Polly Barton

8 —
The Transparent Labyrinth
Keiichirō Hirano
Translated by Kerim Yasar